WALT DISNEY'S
SNOW WHITE
AND THE SEVEN DWARFS

Retold by **CYNTHIA RYLANT**

Pictures by **GUSTAF TENGGREN**

 PRESS

New York

Printed in China
First Edition
1 3 5 7 9 10 8 6 4 2
Library of Congress Cataloging-in-Publication Data on file.

Hand lettering by Leah Palmer Preiss

Colorization of art on pages 17, 20, 23, and 33 by Andrew Phillipson

ISBN 978-1-4231-1861-9

WALT DISNEY'S
SNOW WHITE
AND THE SEVEN DWARFS

I T IS WHEN WE ARE MOST lost that we sometimes find our truest friends.

This is the story of Snow White.

Once a gentle queen so deeply longed for a daughter that she could even see the child in her mind: a beautiful girl with hair coal black, lips ruby red, and skin snow white.

Life listened to the queen's yearning, and it blessed her with the child of her dreams: Snow White. But the queen soon died, leaving the infant behind.

Snow White's father, the King, wanted a new queen to sit by his side. So he married a very beautiful woman. She was now the Queen.

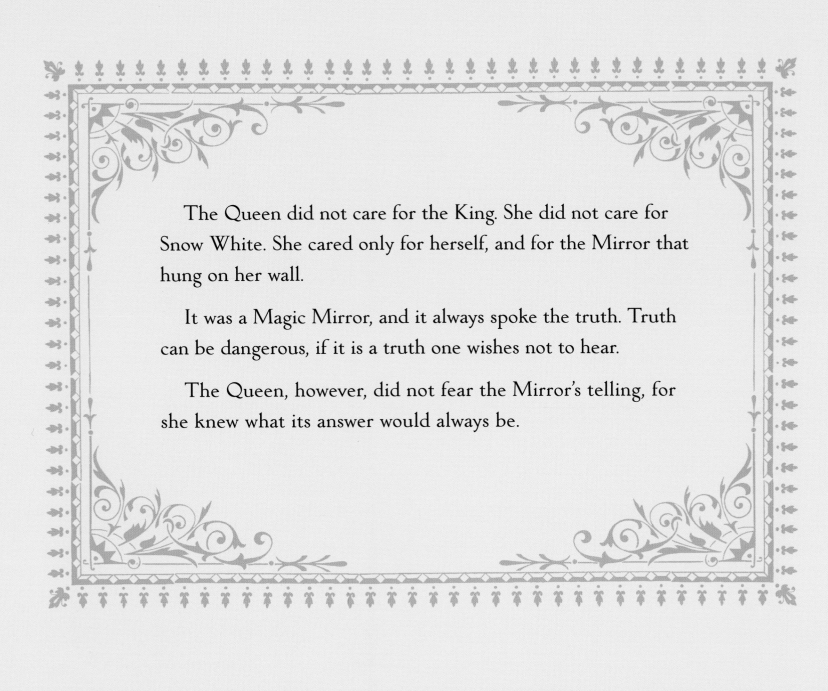

The Queen did not care for the King. She did not care for Snow White. She cared only for herself, and for the Mirror that hung on her wall.

It was a Magic Mirror, and it always spoke the truth. Truth can be dangerous, if it is a truth one wishes not to hear.

The Queen, however, did not fear the Mirror's telling, for she knew what its answer would always be.

Each day, in love with only herself, the Queen asked the Mirror:

> Magic Mirror on the wall,
> Who is the fairest one of all?

And each day, she was given the answer for which she hungered:

> You are the fairest one of all.

Life went on and the child Snow White grew and found many things to love. She loved the small birds in the cherry trees. She loved the deer beside the brook. She even loved the little mice asleep in the forest.

But those with an evil heart seem to have a talent for destroying anything beautiful which is about to bloom. So it was that one day the Queen consulted the Magic Mirror, and Snow White's life was forever changed.

When asked who was the fairest of them all, the Magic Mirror described a girl with hair coal black, lips ruby red, and skin snow white.

The Mirror had spoken the truth. And the truth was dangerous.

The wicked Queen determined there and then to destroy Snow White.

As fate would have it, a young Prince was traveling through the kingdom at this time. He heard someone singing near a wishing well. It was Snow White. The moment he saw her, he loved her.

The Prince found the courage to speak to the girl, but Snow White was shy and soon ran away.

The Prince was determined to one day find her again. But he did not know that Snow White's life was about to take a terrible turn.

royal hunter was commanded by the Queen to take Snow White deep into the forest, kill her, and bring back her heart.

But the hunter could not bring himself to do the terrible deed.

Instead, he told Snow White the truth: that no one could save her from the Queen. He would kill a wild boar for its heart instead. And Snow White must run.

Snow White ran and ran through the dark wood. She was so frightened that it seemed to her even the trees wished her dead.

But Snow White was not long lost, for the little birds and gentle deer of the wood intervened and led her to a small stone cottage.

Snow White knocked, but no one answered. She went in. It was a cozy home but quite messy, with seven little unmade beds.

Snow White thought perhaps it would be all right to stay if she tidied up. She went to work, and her new forest friends helped her, each and every one.

When all was quite in order, Snow White yawned. She was so tired. She lay down on the little beds and fell asleep.

oon, the seven residents of that little cottage finished up their day's work and began the march home. They were Dwarfs who mined the mountains for diamonds.

But as they approached the cottage, the Dwarfs saw candlelight through the windows. Who was there, they wondered.

The Dwarfs went inside and found Snow White asleep. When she awoke, Snow White told them her story.

By the end of her telling, they loved her. How could they not? The Dwarfs had not known gentleness and beauty for a very long time.

They had not even known real happiness.

Snow White changed all that. She brought the Dwarfs music and dancing and days and nights of laughter.

She taught them how to be tidy. Even the grumpiest among them learned to wash his hands before supper.

Snow White opened up their hearts. And as much as they loved her, she loved them in return.

The Dwarfs worried terribly, though, about the Queen. They worried when they were deep in their mine where they could not protect Snow White, who was waiting for them to come home.

The Dwarfs were right to worry. For back at the palace, the Queen was consulting her Mirror.

Magic Mirror on the wall,
Who is the fairest one of all?

And the Magic Mirror, the oracle of truth, told her:
Snow White is the fairest one of all.

Then it told the Queen exactly where Snow White was, very much alive.

There are no words vile enough to describe the Queen's bitter rage. She prepared a poison.

When the wicked want to bring down the innocent, they aim for a loving heart.

The Queen disguised herself as a peddler and walked into the forest.

In the cottage, Snow White
was baking a pie.

When the peddler knocked,
Snow White took pity upon her.
She gave the peddler a piece of
silver for a beautiful red apple.

Snow White bit into the apple
and then fell to the floor, dead.

The Dwarfs came home and saw what had happened. When the Queen tried to escape, the Dwarfs gave chase. Fleeing from them, the terrible Queen plunged over a cliff and was heard from no more.

The Dwarfs returned home. They knew they must bury Snow White. But there was not the darkness of death in her face. She looked too lovely to be laid in the ground.

So the dwarfs carved a crystal coffin. They carefully placed Snow White inside, for themselves and all the forest creatures to see.

But Snow White's story was not yet over. . . .

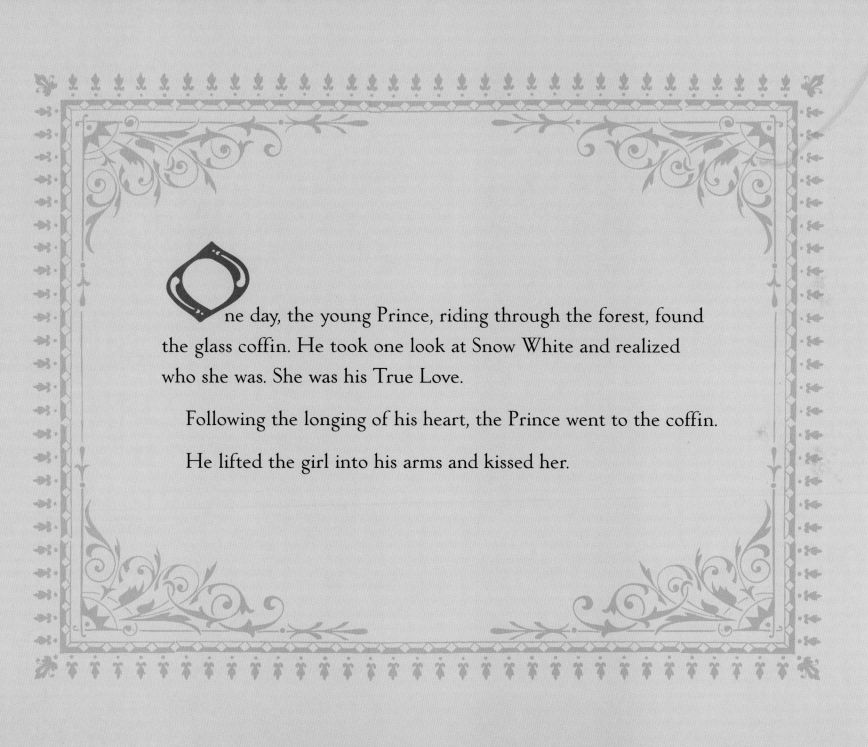

One day, the young Prince, riding through the forest, found the glass coffin. He took one look at Snow White and realized who she was. She was his True Love.

Following the longing of his heart, the Prince went to the coffin.

He lifted the girl into his arms and kissed her.

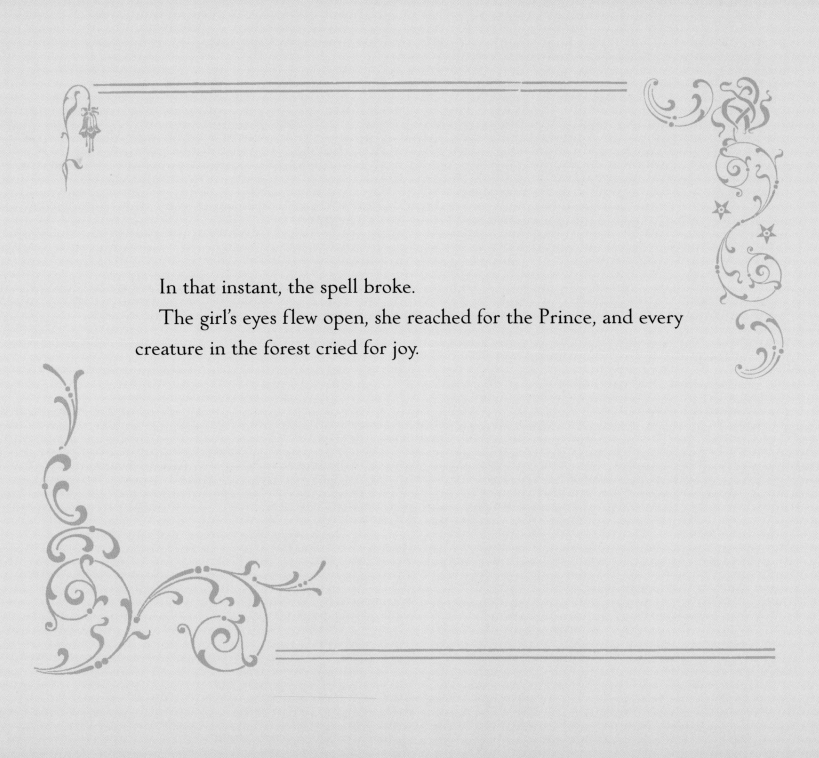

In that instant, the spell broke.

The girl's eyes flew open, she reached for the Prince, and every creature in the forest cried for joy.

Many stories in life have a happy ending, and this is one of them.

Through the magic of love, Snow White was reborn. With seven faithful friends at her side, she married her handsome Prince.

They lived in love ever after.

The End